The Littles
Go on a Hike

Adapted by **Teddy Slater**
from *THE LITTLES TAKE A TRIP*
by **John Peterson**
Illustrated by **Jacqueline Rogers**

SCHOLASTIC INC.
New York Toronto London Auckland Sydney
Mexico City New Delhi Hong Kong Buenos Aires

Cousin Dinky Little was a glider pilot.

He delivered the mail

to tiny people

all over the Big Valley.

Lots of those letters
were from Lucy Little
to Tina Small. And just as many
were from Tina to Lucy.

The two pen pals were

both eight years old.

They were both about

three inches tall.

And they both had

nice long tails.

But even though

they were best friends,

Lucy and Tina

had never even met.

Lucy's family lived

in tiny secret rooms

inside the walls of

Mr. and Mrs. Bigg's house.

The Smalls lived

a whole block away!

More than anything,

Lucy wanted to visit Tina.

But it would take all day

just to get there.

"Oh, please, can't I visit Tina?"

Lucy begged.

"We never go anywhere,"

said her brother, Tom.

"It sounds like a fine

adventure to me,"

said Uncle Pete.

"It sounds dangerous
to me!" said Mrs. Little.
"A tiny person could get
lost in the great outdoors.
And there are wild animals
out there."

"Don't worry," said Cousin Dinky.

"I know the way.

And I'm not afraid of mice

and squirrels.

I'd take you all in my glider,

but it only has two seats.

So, we'll have to walk."

"All right," said Mr. Little,

"but I'm coming, too."

"Hooray!" Lucy shouted.

"We can go tomorrow!"

"I'll stay home with Granny

and Baby Betsy," Mrs. Little said.

The next day, the five Littles

got ready for the long hike.

They all had weapons in case

they met any wild animals.

Lucy's weapon was a jar of pepper.

"Ah-choo!" said Uncle Pete.

"Keep that away from me.

Pepper makes me sneeze."

"It makes everyone sneeze,"

Lucy said with a grin.

"Even wild animals.

And when they sneeze, they can't attack."

Outside the Biggs' door,

Tom climbed a lilac bush.

From there he could see

all the way

down the street.

Littles' house

"The coast is clear,"

Tom called down.

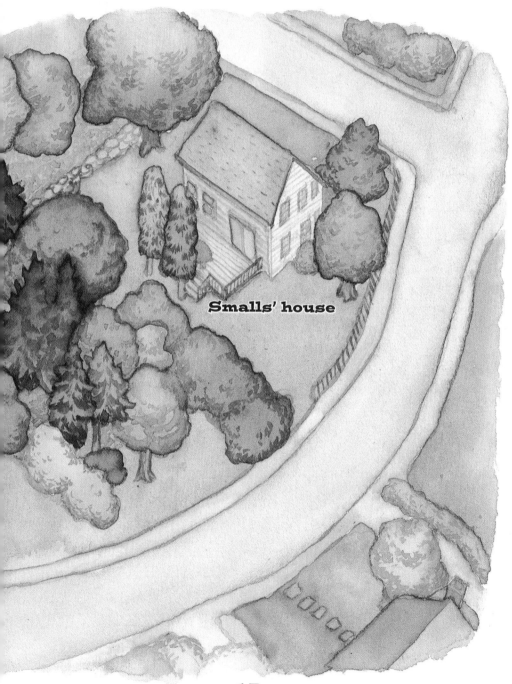

Smalls' house

Cousin Dinky led the way
past Mrs. Bigg's rosebush,
around the walnut tree,
and over the rock wall.

By noon, the Littles

had hiked all the way

across the Biggs' yard.

They plopped down to rest.

Suddenly, they heard
a loud *WHOOSH*
above them.
A dark, scary shadow
fell over the ground.

Lucy looked up and gasped.

A huge bird was

swooping down on Tom.

It dug its claws into

his backpack and started

lifting him into the air.

Mr. Little and Uncle Pete

drew their swords.

But the bird stayed

just out of reach.

Cousin Dinky shot an arrow.

The strong wind blew it away.

Wings fluttered.

Feathers flew.

But the bird did not

let go of Tom.

Lucy held the pepper jar

over her head

and gave it a shake.

SWISH!

A gust of wind blew the pepper

into the bird's face.

The bird shook its head.

It blinked its eyes.

It sneezed and sneezed,

and sneezed some more.

Then it let go of Tom

and flew away.

The Littles set off again.

Late in the day, it began

to rain.

Everyone ducked under

a daisy until the sun

came out again.

By the time the Littles

reached the Smalls' house,

it was getting dark.

Tina Small gave Lucy Little
a big hug.
"I can't believe you're
really here!" she cried.

At dinner that night,

Cousin Dinky told the Smalls

about Lucy's brave deed.

"Hooray for Lucy,"

everyone cried.

Everyone but Uncle Pete. . . .

He just said, "Ah-CHOO!"